Nothing But Trouble

COME ON...YOU DON'T *REALLY* WANT TO READ THIS BOOK, DO YOU? I MEAN, I'M SURE IT'S VERY INACCURATE. IT'S PROBABLY FULL OF LIES AND STORIES ABOUT HOW I CAN NEVER DO ANYTHING RIGHT AND THAT ALL MY PLANS ARE SO SILLY AND...AND...

ADAPTED BY JOHN GREEN

BASED ON THE SERIES CREATED BY
DAN POVENMIRE & JEFF "SWAMPY" MARSH

Disney PRESS
NEW YORK

LIBRARY OF CONGRESS CATALOG CARD NUMBER ON FILE.
ISBN 978-1-4231-2440-5
FIRST EDITION
1 3 5 7 9 10 8 6 4 2
PRINTED IN THE UNITED STATES OF AMERICA
G658-7729-4-10105

FOR MORE DISNEY PRESS FUN, VISIT WWW.DISNEYBOOKS.COM
VISIT DISNEYCHANNEL.COM

SUMMER VACATION! THERE'S A WHOLE LOT OF STUFF TO DO BEFORE SCHOOL STARTS, AND *PHINEAS AND FERB* PLAN TO DO IT ALL! MAYBE THEY'LL BUILD A ROCKET, OR FIND FRANKENSTEIN'S BRAIN...WHATEVER THEY DO, THEY'RE SURE TO ANNOY THEIR SISTER, *CANDACE*. MEANWHILE, THEIR FAMILY PET, *PERRY* THE PLATYPUS, LEADS A DOUBLE LIFE AS AGENT P, FACING OFF AGAINST THE DEVIOUS *DR. DOOFENSHMIRTZ!*

"DAY OF THE LIVING GELATIN!"

AS PRESIDENT OF THE HEALTHY DESSERT CLUB--

--I DECLARE THAT NOTHING SAYS "LOW CALORIE, NONFAT" MORE THAN GELATIN.

YOU WOULDN'T HAVE STARTED THIS CLUB BECAUSE GELATIN IS JEREMY'S FAVORITE DESSERT, WOULD YOU?

WHAT? N-NO.

EW, *GROSS.*

PHINEAS AND FERB! YOUR SMELLY RODENT-PET IS GERMING UP THE CABINETS.

WHERE *ARE* THOSE TWO?

RIGHT HERE, CANDACE.

BUT HOW--HOW DID YOU GET THERE--WHERE YOU ARE--SO FAST?!?

OH, WE WERE JUST PUTTING THE FINISHING TOUCHES ON OUR MOLECULAR TRANSPORTER. WOULD YOU LIKE TO TRY?

DO I *LOOK* LIKE SOMEONE WHO WANTS THEIR MOLECULES TRANSPORTED?

NOW, GET THAT STINKY PET OUT OF OUR CABINETS AND GO SCRAMBLE YOUR MOLECULES SOMEWHERE ELSE.

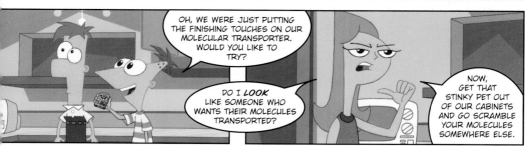

WOULD YOU GUYS LIKE TO TRY SOME OF OUR GELATIN?

NO, WAIT. THEY'LL JUST END UP DOING SOMETHING WEIRD AND RUIN THE PARTY.

HOW IS SHARING GELATIN WITH THEM GONNA RUIN THE PARTY?

SOME... ...HOW?

YOU WANT CHERRY OR GRAPE?

GRAPE, PLEASE!

IT'S AS FUN TO EAT AS THE CRAZY, FUN THINGS YOU CAN DO WITH IT!

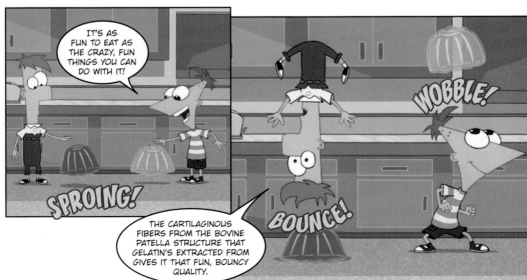

SPROING!

THE CARTILAGINOUS FIBERS FROM THE BOVINE PATELLA STRUCTURE THAT GELATIN'S EXTRACTED FROM GIVES IT THAT FUN, BOUNCY QUALITY.

WOBBLE!

BOUNCE!

WHAT DID I TELL YOU? WEIRD. NOW, LET THE PROFESSIONAL HANDLE THIS BEFORE IT GETS OUTTA HAND.

WHY DON'T YOU MAKE YOUR *OWN* GELATIN AND LEAVE US ALONE.

FERB, I KNOW WHAT WE'RE GONNA DO TODAY.

BYE, CANDACE.

WAIT! I'M NOT FINISHED! STAY AWAY FROM ME AND MY FRIENDS AND MY GELATIN THAT I DON'T WANT *RUINED* WITH YOUR *RUINY RUINNESS.* HMPH!!

WHAT?

SOON...

HEY, ISABELLA. THANKS FOR LETTING US USE YOUR SWIMMING POOL AS THE LARGEST GELATIN MOLD EVER.

YOU BET.

GELATIN

FERB, RELEASE THE GELATIN MIX.

RRRUMBLE

GELATIN

RELEASE!

OOH, OOH, OOH! MAY I ADD SOME OF *MY* FAVORITE FLAVOR?

SURE, BUDDY.

HEE-HEE-HEE!

STIRRING TEAM, COMMENCE MIXING OPERATIONS.

AYE-AYE.

HEY, WHERE'S PERRY?

GOOD QUESTION, PHINEAS! WHERE *IS* PERRY?!?

GRAB!

WHOOOSH!

AH, THERE YOU ARE, AGENT P.

DOOFENSHMIRTZ HAS SENT YOU A VIDEO MESSAGE. TAKE A LOOK.

OH, HELLO, PERRY THE PLATYPUS! I'M SURE YOU'RE GETTING THIS. I-I WAS *HOPING* YOU WOULD STOP BY TODAY FOR SOME *TEA.*

SEE, I'VE GOT ALL THESE LITTLE *TEA THINGS* SET OUT AND READY, AND, UM...

AND, P-PLEASE USE THE *FRONT ENTRANCE,* PERRY THE PLATYPUS, BECAUSE, UH...

...BECAUSE ALL THE OTHER ENTRANCES DON'T WORK TODAY. SO BYE-BYE. I'LL SEE YOU LATER TODAY.

COMING IN THROUGH THE FRONT ENTRANCE.

SO YOU SEE, DOOFENSHMIRTZ HAS INVITED YOU TO TEA. WE DON'T KNOW WHAT IT COULD POSSIBLY MEAN.

WE THINK--BUT DON'T HOLD US TO THIS-- WE THINK THAT MAYBE, *JUST MAYBE*, IT COULD BE A TRAP.

WE DO, HOWEVER, LIKE TO GIVE PEOPLE THE BENEFIT OF THE DOUBT, SO TRY TO HAVE FUN. *MONOGRAM OUT.*

AS PERRY RACES OFF FOR TEA...

HOW'S IT LOOKIN', PHINEAS?

LOOKS GOOD. AND JUDGING BY MY CHRONOMETER, IT SHOULD BE JUST ABOUT TIME. THERE'S ONLY ONE THING TO DO NOW.

YOU MEAN TEST THE RESILIENCY OF OUR CARTILAGINOUS COLLUSION WITH VIGOROUS APPLICATION OF WEIGHT AND VELOCITY?

EXACTLY. LET'S JUMP ON IT!

BWONG!

WHEE!

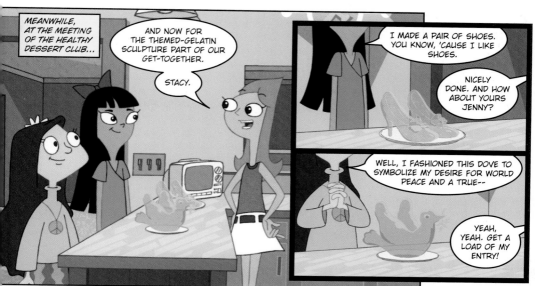

YEAH, COME ON.

NAH, IT'S OKAY. GO AHEAD.

BWONG!

THAT DOES LOOK KINDA FUN.

MAYBE I SHOULD...

...TOTALLY BUST THEM FOR THIS!!

MEANWHILE...

Doofenshmirtz Evil Inc.

THIS IS NICE, HUH?

YOU KNOW, I WAS THINKING THE OTHER DAY ABOUT HOW MUCH BETTER YOU WOULD BE AS AN *ALLY*.

SO I-- CREATED *THIS!*

beep!

I CALL IT MY *TURN-EVERYTHING-EVIL-INATOR*. NOW, YOU JUST SIT STILL. OKAY, GREAT. YOU KNOW, AFTER I TURN YOU EVIL, WE CAN USE IT TO CREATE A WHOLE ARMY OF EVIL MINIONS. WON'T THAT BE FUN?

HOLD STILL.

ZAP!

ZAP!

ZAP!

HEY!

I'M BEGINNING TO THINK YOU DON'T WANT TO BE ALLIES AT ALL.

I'M TRYING NOT TO TAKE IT PERSONAL.

ZAP!

ZAP!

GRAAR!

GRAAR!

WHO ADDED THE EVIL FLAVOR?

IT'S CURRY.

IT'S NOT *INHERENTLY* EVIL.

MAYBE A LITTLE SPICY.

OKAY, I'M GOING HOME.

GRAAR!

AIEEEEE!!

WHAT THE--?

WAIT TILL MOM SEES *THIS!*

GRAAR!

gulp!

YOU GUYS ARE *SO BUSTED!*

WELL, I GUESS WE'D BETTER RESCUE CANDACE.

BUT HOW DO WE FIGHT A GELATIN MONSTER?

WE'LL BEAT HIM THE SAME WAY WE CREATED HIM-- WITH *WATER.*

AND THIS ROPE MIGHT COME IN HANDY, TOO.

TO THE MUNITIONS DEPOT!

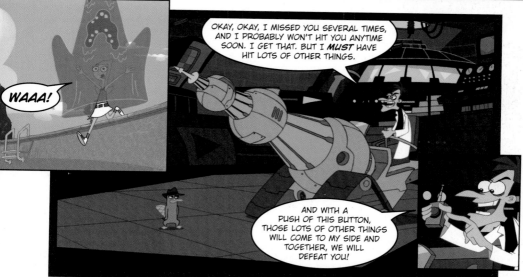

FOR CANDACE, OUR NEIGHBORHOOD, AND ALL THE GOOD GELATIN LEFT IN THE WORLD!

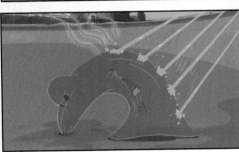

MASTER?

IT'S WORKING. HE'S MELTING DOWN THE DRAIN!

HOORAY!

I HAVE *GOT* TO REEXAMINE MY LIFE.

HERE THEY COME, PERRY THE PLATYPUS! HERE THEY COME, ALL OF MY MINIONS! HA-HA-HA-HA!

I COU-- I...

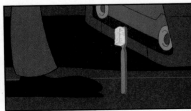

NOW YOU CAN *KOWTOW* BEFORE MY CARTILAGINOUS CREATION. IT'S SO *CORRUPT* AND *CANTANKEROUS* AND *CARNIVOROUS* AND, UH...

...UH, LOW IN *CALORIES* AND CA--CA...COW. COUCH. HM...AH, THAT'S ALL I GOT.

PERRY HAS A PLAN-- AND TAKES EXPERT AIM...

clink!

SPOOOSH!!!

bzzt bzzt bzzt

KABOOM!

MY TURN-EVERYTHING-EVIL-INATOR! *NO!*

RAARG!

SO KIDS, ARE YOU ENJOYING YOUR VISIT TO ENGLAND?

THERE'S NOTHING TO DO, GRANDMA.

WHAT? WHY DON'T YOU READ MY OLD *SHERLOCK HOLMES* BOOKS? I'VE GOT THE WHOLE COLLECTION RIGHT HERE.

GEE, THANKS MRS. FLETCHER.

DINNER'S AT 1900. THAT'S 7:00 FOR YOU YANKS.

AH, YES, READING. THAT'S WHAT THEY DID BEFORE THEY INVENTED *FUN.*

I HEARD THAT.

WELL, IT'S BETTER THAN NOTHING. MM? MMHMM. HMM...

THE NEXT MORNING...

OKAY, IS EVERYBODY READY?

WE'RE GOING TO TAKE YOU KIDS TO SEE THE *LONDON EYE.* IT'S ONE OF THE *LARGEST* FERRIS WHEELS IN THE ENTIRE *UNIVERSE.*

COOL.

GIRLS, ARE YOU READY?

WAI--WAI-- ALMOST FINISHED.

CANDACE, YOU STAYED UP ALL NIGHT JUST TO FINISH THAT *BOOK?*

NO, NO. WE FINISHED THE WHOLE *COLLECTION.*

HEY, WHERE'S PERRY?

OH, THERE HE IS.

SEE YOU LATER, OLD BOY. BE GOOD NOW.

GOOD MORNING, AGENT P.

DOOFENSHMIRTZ IS UP TO NO GOOD HERE IN THE U.K.*

*U.K.--UNITED KINGDOM!

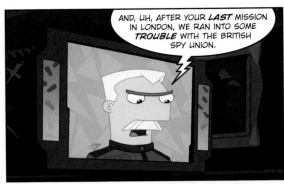
AND, UH, AFTER YOUR *LAST* MISSION IN LONDON, WE RAN INTO SOME *TROUBLE* WITH THE BRITISH SPY UNION.

SO JOINING YOU TODAY IS *AGENT DOUBLE O-O*, AND JOINING *ME* TODAY IS THE LOVELY INSPECTOR INITIALS.

DOUBLE O-O, YOU AND AGENT P WILL BE ASSIGNED THE SAME MISSION AGAINST DR. DOOFENSHMIRTZ.

YOU REALIZE THIS MAN IS A PLATYPUS?

THEY'RE AMERICAN, DOUBLE O-O. JUST BE GLAD IT'S A *MAMMAL.*

WELL, GO GET HIM, AGENT P.

WHAT? THAT'S IT? NO FILES? NO LOCATION? NO CONTACT? WHAT KIND OF A MISSION *IS* THIS?

HMMPH! IT WAS ENOUGH FOR THE MAMMAL.

HEY, WHERE'S PHINEAS?

HERE ARE YOUR TICKETS FOR THE LONDON EYE.

DAD AND GRANDPA ARE GOING TO THE INTERNATIONAL HAGGIS FESTIVAL. WE'LL PICK YOU UP AROUND 4:15. BYE, KIDS.

HAVE FUN.

BYE.

CANDACE, YOU KNOW WHAT? FERB AND I WILL MEET YOU BACK HERE LATER. SEE YA!

BYE, GUYS!

DID YOU HEAR THAT? EVEN IN *ENGLAND*, MY BROTHERS HAVE SOME *SCHEME* PLANNED.

HOW CAN YOU TELL?

YOU DON'T HAVE TO BE SHERLOCK HOLMES TO--

OOH, STACY, THAT'S *IT!* WHO DID WE STAY UP ALL NIGHT LEARNING ABOUT? WHO IS THE *TOTAL KING* OF BUSTING?

SHERLOCK HOLMES?

YES. MAYBE I CAN FINALLY BUST THE BOYS ONCE AND FOR ALL IF I USE HOLMES' METHOD OF DEDUCTION!

COME ON, THIS WILL BE FUN! YOU COULD BE DR. WATSON!

ELSEWHERE...

THAT'S IT.

WE'RE TAKING *MY* CAR.

BY USING HOLMESY DEDUCTION, WE'LL BE ONE STEP AHEAD OF THE BOYS.

WE CAN GET MOM AND FINALLY SHOW HER--

AUTO SPARES

SPARES SERVICE

OOH! THERE THEY ARE.

NOW, WHY ARE THEY GOING INTO AN AUTO-PARTS STORE?

ALL RIGHT, WATSON. HERE'S WHERE THE DEDUCING BEGINS. THEY'VE...ACQUIRED A FLEET OF AUTOMOBILES, AND THEY'RE IN THERE BUYING A BUNCH OF LITTLE AIR FRESHENERS FOR THEM...OR... THEY'RE BUYING MOTOR OIL FOR THEIR *GIANT ROBOT!* WHAT DO YOU THINK, STACE?

STACE?

WHAT?

MEANWHILE, BENEATH BIG BEN...

knock knock

PERRY THE PLATYPUS!

OH, WHO'S YOUR LITTLE FRIEND HERE?

I'M AGENT DOUBLE O-O, FROM HER MAJESTY'S SECRET SERVICE.

DOUBLE O-O? ISN'T THAT JUST *TRIPLE O?*

NO, THAT'S *NOT* HOW YOU SAY IT.

IT SPELLS "OOO" DOESN'T IT?

IT'S JUST *DOUBLE O-O.*

HE'S *P* AND YOU'RE *OOO.* SO TOGETHER YOU SPELL...

NO, THEY'RE NOT "O'S," THEY'RE *ZEROS.* ALL RIGHT?

I WAS JUST GOING TO SAY "OOOP." LOOKS LIKE I STRUCK A NERVE THERE. *ANYWAY,* SHALL WE MOVE ON?

click!

I MUST APOLOGIZE. ALL OF MY TRAPS ARE PLATYPUS-SIZED.

CLAMP!

CLAMP!

WHAT ABOUT *THIS* THEN?

OH, THAT.

YOU SEE, AS I GET OLDER, I FIND IT'S HARDER AND HARDER TO READ MY SMALL, LITTLE WRISTWATCH.

SO I WILL LAUNCH BIG BEN INTO SPACE...

WHEEEE!

...AND FLY IT ALL THE WAY TO THE TRI-STATE AREA.

LA, LA, LA. HERE I AM. LA, LA, LA.

I JUST WOKE UP, AND I WANT TO KNOW WHAT TIME IT IS.

YES, I AM A GENIUS!

SO THAT... THAT'S YOUR WHOLE PLAN?

WELL, IN A NUTSHELL, YES. WHAT DO YOU THINK?

AM I ON ONE OF THOSE HIDDEN-CAMERA SHOWS?

YOU REALIZE YOU COULD JUST *BUY* A BIGGER WATCH. OR MAYBE A *WALL CLOCK*?

YES, BUT THEN I WOULD HAVE TO DRIVE TO A *STORE* AND FIND A *PARKING SPACE.* THEN YOU HAVE TO CHOOSE FROM, LIKE, *DOZENS* OF STYLES.

IT JUST SEEMED LIKE SO MUCH *WORK.* THIS WILL BE MUCH LESS COMPLICATED.

BACK TO SHERLOCK AND WATSON...

EXCUSE ME, SIR. WERE THESE TWO BOYS IN HERE EARLIER?

WELL, THEM TWO THINGS WERE HANGIN' ABOUT, AND THEY HAD A BIT OF A BUTCHERS, AND, UH, WHIRLS AROUND THE BACK AND CARTED OFF SOME OLD BANGERS THAT I DIDN'T NEED.

OY, AREN'T THEY A BIT HAIRLESS FOR THEM KINDA BUSHIES?

UH... STACY?

I'M WORKING ON IT. AH. HE SAID, "THEY WERE HERE. THEY CARTED AWAY SOME JUNK FROM OUT BACK." AND, "AREN'T THEY A LITTLE YOUNG TO BE DOING THAT?"

COCKNEY FOR TOURISTS

YES. YES, THEY ARE.

AHA. IT'S CRAWLING WITH CLUES OUT HERE.

HMM, LOOK AT THESE CIRCULAR INDENTATIONS IN THE DIRT. AND THE SUBTLE SCENT OF RUBBER IN THE AIR. BY JOVE, STACY, *WHAT COULD IT BE?*

UH, FREE TIRES?

FREE TIRES

MAYBE, MAYBE. WE NEED MORE CLUES.

FIRST CLUE--TIRES. SECOND CLUE--PINEAPPLE.

THIRD CLUE--BUTTER.

FOURTH CLUE--PIPES.

STACY, I THINK I'M CLOSE TO FIGURING IT OUT!

CLUNK!

PSSHHH... RUMBLE RUMBLE

MEANWHILE...

WELL, I'M GOING UP TO THE TOP OF THE TOWER.

I'M SURE YOU TWO WILL HAVE A HOT TIME TOGETHER. HA-HA-HA-HA!

DON'T WORRY, AGENT P.

I'LL HAVE US OUT OF THESE BEFORE YOU KNOW IT.

UNDERNEATH BIG BEN...

JUST A FEW MORE MINUTES.

beep!

CLANK!

YOWCH!

OH, THERE YOU GO. GOOD THING I HAD THE WATCH-LASER.

DOOFENSHMIRTZ TOOK THE STAIRS...

...BUT IF WE WORK OUR WAY UP THROUGH THE INNER MECHANISMS OF THE CLOCK, HE'LL NEVER SEE US COMING.

HUP!

HUP!

HUP!

HUP!

ding!

AT STREET LEVEL...

WHOA! CANDACE, YOU'RE AMAZING, YOU TOTALLY FIGURED IT OUT!

YEAH, I GUESS I DID. NOW, ON TO THE *BUSTING*.

WHEE!

NEXT!

WOO-HOO!

PHINEAS!

I FIGURED YOU GUYS WERE UP TO SOMETHING.

OH, HEY, GUYS! DO YOU LIKE IT?

THE TIRES, THE PIPES. I SEE WHAT THOSE WERE FOR...

...BUT WHAT WAS WITH THE PINEAPPLE?

OH, THAT WAS FOR FERB. HE WAS HUNGRY.

OH, AND THE BUTTER, TOO, HUH?

NO, NO.

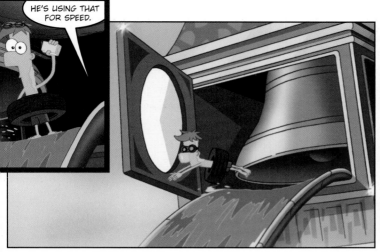

HE'S USING THAT FOR SPEED.

IT'S A NEW WORLD RECORD!

MOM'S GONNA *FLIP* WHEN SHE HEARS ABOUT THIS.

CLAMP!

HELLO?

GARBBIBLGLUBBLEGURGLEBLARG!

SOMEONE WITH A THICK COCKNEY ACCENT. WRONG NUMBER.

THE END!